Dear Parents and Educators,

Welcome to Penguin Young Readers! As parents and educators, you know that each child develops at his or her own pace—in terms of speech, critical thinking, and, of course, reading. Penguin Young Readers recognizes this fact. As a result, each Penguin Young Readers book is assigned a traditional easy-to-read level (1–4) as well as a Guided Reading Level (A–P). Both of these systems will help you choose the right book for your child. Please refer to the back of each book for specific leveling information. Penguin Young Readers features esteemed authors and illustrators, stories about favorite characters, fascinating nonfiction, and more!

Nina, Nina Ballerina

LEVEL 2

GUIDED READING LEVEL G

This book is perfect for a **Progressing Reader** who:

- can figure out unknown words by using picture and context clues;
- can recognize beginning, middle, and ending sounds;
- can make and confirm predictions about what will happen in the text; and
- can distinguish between fiction and nonfiction.

Here are some **activities** you can do during and after reading this book:

- Comprehension: Answer the following questions about the story.
    - Who is the queen butterfly in the big dance show?
    - What happens to Nina when she is in the park?
    - Why does Nina cry after the doctor puts a cast on her arm?
    - How does Nina's mom recognize her onstage?
- Character's Feelings: Nina has lots of different feelings in this book. For example, she is worried when she thinks her mother won't recognize her in the ballet show, and she is nervous before she finally goes onstage. How do you think Nina will feel after the ballet show?

Remember, sharing the love of reading with a child is the best gift you can give!

—Bonnie Bader, EdM
Penguin Young Readers program

*Penguin Young Readers are leveled by independent reviewers applying the standards developed by Irene Fountas and Gay Su Pinnell in *Matching Books to Readers: Using Leveled Books in Guided Reading*, Heinemann, 1999.

For Dad—JOC

To Marja—Thanks for the X-ray.
With love—DD

PENGUIN YOUNG READERS
Published by the Penguin Group
Penguin Group (USA) Inc., 375 Hudson Street, New York, New York 10014, USA

USA | Canada | UK | Ireland | Australia | New Zealand | India | South Africa | China
Penguin Books Ltd, Registered Offices: 80 Strand, London WC2R 0RL, England

For more information about the Penguin Group visit penguin.com

 First published in 1993 by Grosset & Dunlap, an imprint of Penguin Group (USA) Inc. Published in 2013 by Penguin Young Readers, an imprint of Penguin Group (USA) Inc., 345 Hudson Street, New York, New York 10014. Manufactured in China.

Library of Congress Control Number: 92024465

ISBN 978-0-448-40511-7

10 9 8 7 6 5 4

PENGUIN YOUNG READERS

LEVEL 2 PROGRESSING READER

Nina, Nina Ballerina

by Jane O'Connor
illustrated by DyAnne DiSalvo

Penguin Young Readers
An Imprint of Penguin Group (USA) Inc.

Nina wants to be
a ballerina.

Every week

she goes to dance class.

She can stand on one leg.

But not like Sara can.

She can

do a split.

But not like

Sara can.

Sara is the best in the class.

Soon there will be

a big dance show.

Nina's class will be butterflies.

Miss Dawn picks Sara

to be the queen butterfly.

Nina does not mind.

Not too much.

That night Nina tells her mom,

"We all get wings

and bug masks.

Sara is lucky.

She is the queen.

She gets a crown.

Sara's mom will know

it's her right away.

But the rest of us

look the same . . .

how will you know it's me?"

Nina's mom gives her a hug.

"Do not worry.

I will know it's you."

But Nina is not so sure.

The next week the kids try on

their wings and masks.

“You are lucky,”

Nina tells Beth.

“Your mom will know you

because you are so tall.”

Then Miss Dawn claps.

The class is ready to start.

“Pretend you have wings,”
Miss Dawn tells the class.
“Pretend you are flitting
from flower to flower.”

Nina does just what
Miss Dawn says.
She tries hard to be
a good butterfly.

Nina goes over the steps

to the dance all day . . .

. . . and all night.

It is the day

before the dance show.

Nina is in the park.

"Watch me flit
from flower to flower,"
Nina says to her friends.

Nina leaps.

She feels like she has wings.

She feels like a butterfly

even if she is not the queen.

“Watch out!” her friends yell.

But it is too late.

Nina falls.

Nina's mom takes her

to the doctor.

Nina's arm is broken!

The doctor puts a cast on it.

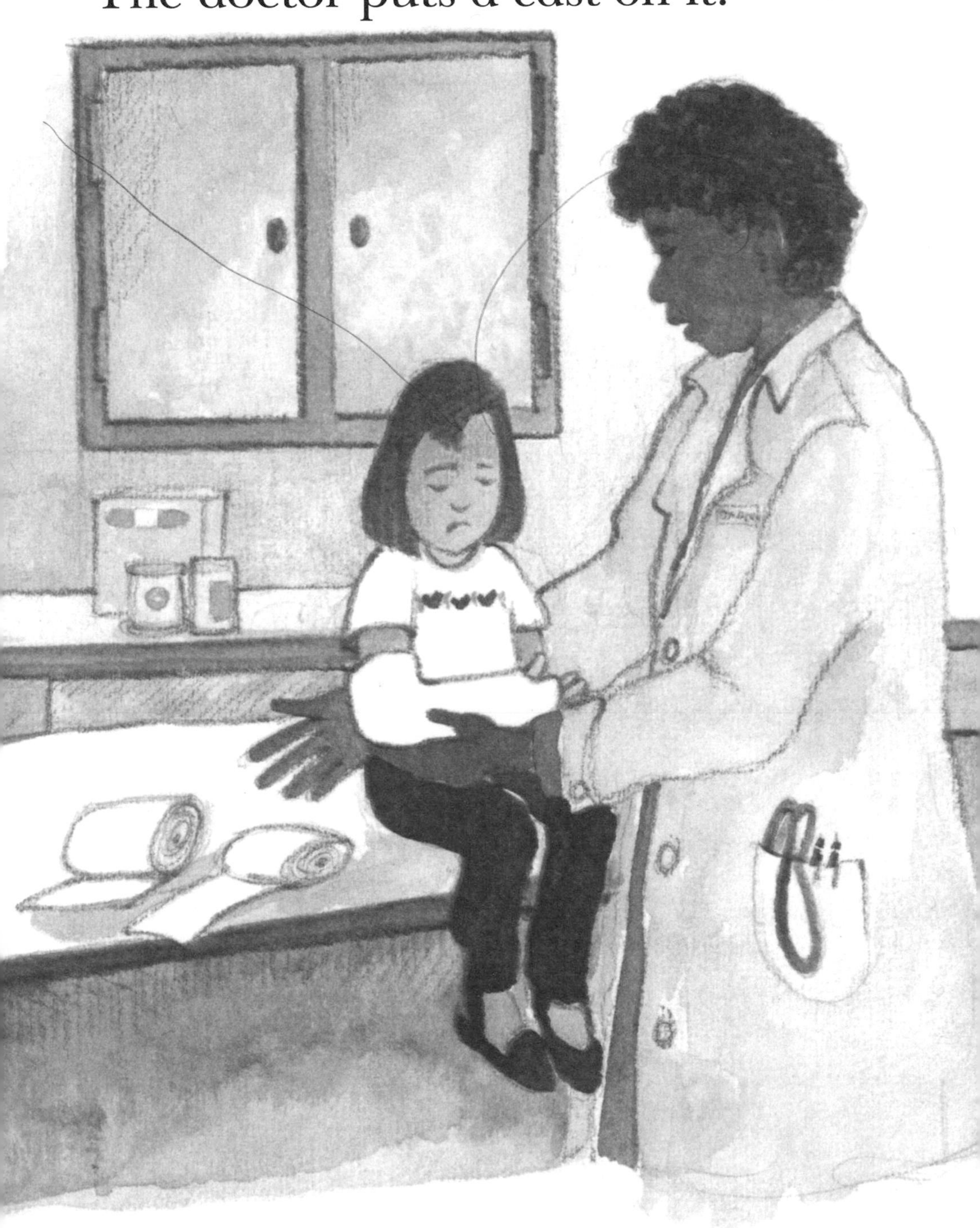

The cast is so heavy.
Nina does not feel like
she has wings anymore.
Nina starts to cry.
"It will stop hurting soon,"
her mom says.
Nina sniffs.
"That is not
why I am crying.
I can't be
in the dance show now!"

"Miss Dawn says you can
still be in the dance.
You will be a butterfly
with a broken wing."

That does not sound
so hot to Nina.
But she does not want
to miss the dance.

It is the next day.

The show is about to start.

Nina's tummy feels like

it is full of butterflies.

The music begins.

“Just do your best,”

Miss Dawn tells the class.

That is just what Nina does.

Can Nina's mom tell which butterfly is Nina?

She sure can!